JEREMY SMITH

(Or Something Like That)

OLIVER FRANCES

Jeremy Smith

(Or Something Like That)

Oliver Frances

Published by Marco A Diaz
Revised Edition by Amanda Mathis
Cover Art by Natasha Padron
Copyright 2023 Marco A Diaz

"Within the enormous depths, fissures disseminated as long limbs entwined around Northern land, whilst prominences rose as laments upon the arid land of the South. It was a sort of irritated creature as Nature came up, bursting out its cholera, the origin of a cataclysm. The irritation of Nature, once it was dissipated, had become a creator God who carved the utmost imposing ridges upon Earth."

The trimmings of the long, refulgent mantle of the God of Light were over the swollen, emerald-coloured arms of the one who protected the city from Neptune's brutal attacks a descendent of nature, and to whom was given the empire in the Creation. Already, the bewildering excitement of the city began to die away, and, by nightfall the pandemonium was becoming a distant note. The ladies of the empire went to their respective dwellings in order to wait for a brand new day.

On the narrow road, which stretched out as far as a marvellous, big chair, the coppery lights of the posts were already on. The wrinkled countenances, drowsy from the scorching liquor and breath pestilent with nicotine, put the thread bags over their hunchbacks to begin their labour at the early hours. Their routine went along with the battle cry: "We get drunk, but we don't bother you!" And the few cars that rode along were similar to the drops left by a vigorous torrent.

On one side of the road were the remains of the patrimony of the city, where the old houses sat with their windows overlooking the road, near where the maiden used to sit and wait for the pretenders who went front of them. And, along the other side, the moderate dimensions of the buildings, one representative characteristic of modernism, lined up.

The gilt iron bars of one of the main doors of the small construction which moulded the corner were witness of the two youth's dignified chatter over the steps outside of the block. One of them grabbed a little stone and placed it into his coarse fingers as he was telling his bosom friend the reason to immigrate to the developed nations.

"Technology belongs to the first world. Over there, everything has to deal with the technological advances. If your idea is behind the times you throw it away immediately. Here, in the third world, we are subject to the rudimentary. In our dictionary is not found the word: technology." The abridged vocabulary used by the Peñon, as the neighbourhood nicknamed him, created a marvellous compendium of outrageous concepts to depict underdevelopment.

"A northern man is apt to development." The Peñon said. "He has inside him the seed of it. That person is open-minded. I mean he accepts new ideas and renew those that he has kept on his mind. Meanwhile, in the Caribbean, the man of the south fights against anything that can put in danger his power. For this reason, he enslaves his citizens through ignorance and misery. So, you can see the torturing impoverishment and misery here."

The long extremity of Mochito's fragile body reached through the plain bars, of the wrought iron door placed over the second step, to clasp it and make it swing from one side to the other.

"Life is easy in the north. Here, your life is martyrdom."

"You believe that everything is not sooner said than done over there. You will be enormously disappointed. That doesn't exist. You belong to the Tropics. We're from here. There is no place for us there. Get used to your town." The young man's words were a stabbing lance, whose fierce point stung the idealist's heart.

"Foolish things… It is the celebrated reason of the third world. I mean the failures'. Look at the actors, who have gone to the north, many of them didn't know how to speak the language. And, as you can see they have made themselves famous and millionaires."

"There is no place for you there," his friend said.

"There's one or I'll do it."

The Peñon threw the hot stone out of his hand. With his sight following its bounce upon the pavement, Mochito asked a question. "How will you get there?"

"Easy... I have to talk my parents into giving me the money to do an English course. So, when I am there I'll look for any way to introduce myself into their society. Don't worry about it. I'll do something… Technology will help me."

"Is it not better to establish a little business with that money, instead of going away to blow it on making a fool of yourself?"

"Look, I am fed up with being in a third world country. I want to live something much better."

Upset by his friend's stupidity, the Peñon ended the deliberation about his progress, his thickset figure leaping to his feet. Pacing up into the shadows, he went to call on his young love, who had turned his nights sleepless.

***

Peñon's celebrated discourse upon the marvellous privileges of the citizens of the first world had came to an end, when he did convince his parents of the benefits of his leaving. The most important reason was learning the English language, to which was added the fortune of being in a land of nobles. Aristocracy was the peculiar characteristic of that nation that distinguished it from the colossus of the north, which had a sort of dominance over the other countries. The Peñon's firmness to take advantage of the opportunity charmed his father, who had the conviction that the tough experience his son was to have on foreign ground would turn him into a man. Although there were enough reasons to bless his departure, Peñon's mother was just against the idea. For her, it was much better for him to do

Oliver Frances

university studies in his own country. The whole thing reminded her of Jules Verne's book Around The World In Eighty Days. However, in very few days, the understanding that some tourist courses and the knowledge of a foreign language would make her son a millionaire achieved her blessing.

Peñon did not waste time on organizing his departure. At the elegant British Council's offices, where the Peñon arrived, the blowzy studies assistant praised the nation as she was telling him all the information regarding the expenses and procedures required to enrol in a university or college. Upon that brilliant way, there were a lot of obstructions. The requirements for a visa were tough, and there was an impediment to his acceptance at university, in accordance with the culture treaty between both countries, any immigrant student had to have at least two years of previous studies at a university in his native land, in order to qualify for a place at an institution of the same educational level. So, the only alternative left was to search for a college whose only admission requisite was to have enough money to afford the studies program. Even though Peñon had never dreamt about encountering this kind of an obstacle, it did not upset his plans. The name of the institution was not important for his country's economic agents; the important thing was to have a degree or certificate from a first-world school. An ideology of that sort, which his parents shared too, belonged to the third world.

***

The refulgent majestic mantle of the God of Light smashing the hollowed turquoise was the only thing Peñon saw, while in the waters of the realm of demigods, Tritons upon sea horses rode over the greenish undulations of tide, and the tearing lashes of the God of Wind's whip were over Mother Nature and the earthly creatures.

A lengthy procession of cars was heading for the airport. An enormous enjoyment surged in the Peñon's heart as he saw the long runway.

His annoyed countenance was among the many in the queue waiting to check luggage in at the desk. As usual, the personnel were deluged with complaints about their slowness in waiting on the travellers and the placement of the tense barriers, which formed a maze. The justification for the chaos was the airline assistants' nationality -Portuguese.

"Look at the French. They have a lineal queue. You can see the separators are lined up. And, this is a mess. They had to be Portuguese - Southern people," The Peñon said to one of his relatives.

The ill comment did bring a reprimand. An elderly woman turning around rebuked the lad.

Oliver Frances

"Don't be offensive, boy! The Portuguese made this country." After these words, the Peñon endured his exasperation mutely.

There was an hour left before departure once the passengers complied with the procedure for boarding the plane, and Peñon's relatives used the time to impart some advice. Their words of wisdom turned out to be a compendium of dangers to avoid, from drug addiction to homosexuality. And, as always, they teased him about romance, a peculiar characteristic of the Latin American at departure.

The natural cause of his mother's heart-sore cry was the advice to get on the aircraft that came from a fine, modulated voice. The long faces of the members of his family and his girlfriend's faint worsened her grief.

The next seven hours of navigation were a festivity because of the amusing occurrences of one of the travellers who was close to the Peñon. He did not understand how to fasten the seat belt, and it was funny to observe him messing about with it. On many occasions, the passenger thanked the stewardess for her willingness to wait on him. The climax of his humorous action occurred when he believed that the rolled hot towel the flight assistant gave him was a ham roll. But the fun was over once the plane reached Lisbon; Peñon had to take another plane to England. The happy faces were exchanged for long ones. There was a hermetic silence on the trip. It was the first world.

On arrival in England, the lad found all the immigrants segregated between European Community members and foreigners. The queues flowed along nicely between official's desks on the side meant for community members, but the stranger's lines moved at a turtle-like pace because of the immigration officials' endless interrogation. The Peñon took an hour and a half to prove that he complied with the nation's legal requirements to get through.

The immense hall outside Customs was eerie for him. He had never seen such a thing before, he understood now that he was in an unknown land -which might well be an unfriendly one. Nevertheless, he did have to fight against adversity until a chance to achieve his aims was thrown at his feet. An elderly man, whose figure was similar to a thin line, approached the lad to ask him. "Do you need a taxi?"

Because the word "Taxi" was used in Portuguese language too, it was the only thing that he understood. "Yes," he said, putting in practice the English he had learned in his high school lessons.

"Where are you going to? Out of London or central London? Don't worry, you will tell me in the car."

Oliver Frances

The grammatical constructions turned out to be harder to understand at every minute went by, so, at that moment, the Peñon felt that the best thing to do was to obviate them by pronouncing the name of the station where he desired to go, before pulling out of his back trousers pocket the famous little book "Do You Want to Learn English in Ten Days?", which he read in twenty days -the first ten to learn and the rest to build up his vocabulary. So, there was no other alternative. He did have to trust the well-mannered gentleman -whose cheeks glowed by the cold breeze.

"Victoria Station... Station Victoria... Victoria..."

On the way, the only word came out of his lips was "yes", with which he replied to any comment made by the chauffeur, who was not a taxi driver, just a somebody in need of money, for he approached the airport to hunt a lost tourist who arrived in the country at midnight. When they got to the station, the gentleman told the Peñon the fare, which he paid with the little money he had already changed. It was nothing to the Peñon. As time went by, the event was no longer valueless when he realized that cost of the ride has been the salary of three workdays in a taxi.

At Victoria, the lad did not perceive the dimension of the hall until he had bought his ticket to go to the destined town. By gestures and some signals accompanied by ill-pronounced English words, he asked a worker where the right boarding platform was. The man, putting himself out, led the Peñon to the right one.

The following day, already in the boarding home, the perceptions of the ruinous house, which once had been a luxurious one, brought over him an enormous ill impression, and disappointment that such a thing could exist in the kingdom. Gloominess had crawled along the narrow, chapped path of the entrance as far as the premises, but he had not been able to observe that dreadful scenery the night before. In his bedroom, he attributed an odd noise to ghostly apparitions, but soon dismissed this theory when he realized that the structure was made to tremble by even a light movement.

During the break time, after his English lessons, the overwhelming deception was whiled away when the Peñon assembled with the Latin Americans and Spaniards all together to talk about their hilarious experiences with the continental people, who were not always agreeable to the Latin company.

Even though the northern people's bad temper was not something lovely, the Peñon was determined to triumph in the battle to accomplish his aims. He saw the future through the mirror of optimism. The view of a new horizon would come along when he had learned

Oliver Frances

the nation's language, and he would remain here until his dying hour. Once the vocals flowed like river waters through a bed, he would know that world.

His mother tongue was just a link to Latin culture, owing to the fact that his chats with the Portuguese and Spaniards in the language school were very common. Anyhow, these talks had never bloomed into any desire to initiate friendship with the other overseas —that is, Latin American- students, because he thought it would be quite illogical for him to approach that part of the third world once he got rid of his backwardness.

It would not be long before his destiny would become completely distinct. Fortune had destined a loot for him. His life was like a vessel navigating through a broad sea -the world. The treasure he sought was conquest of the flower most appreciated by the native of the land, in whose harbour his ship had anchored. To a far away geography the prince had escaped. A pawn was the noble. It was inconceivable to reach the queen's love, but his dedication to her made him obtain it. The whole affair was like a fairy tale, carried out in reality, where the wild horses would be the potent engines of the cars, and the swords the high-tech devices used by contemporary men.

The Peñon was having a stroll along a road when he noticed the figure of an attractive lady trying to start up the engine of her car. As any gentleman would, he approached the desperate woman to offer his help. Obviously, once he fixed the breakdown, the nice creature gave him a lift. In that precise moment, delightful sentiments flourished, and the casual encounter ended in marriage. To his surprise, the gorgeous woman was an aristocrat. Happiness was tied to his life. Even if she were not high born, her heart was so beautiful that she would cooperate with her husband on his laborious enterprises, prosperous businesses that he intended to establish as the Jewish and Italians had done in North America. Success was inscribed in golden words on the pages of his future book.

Meanwhile, he was contented with laughable situations as a consequence of his lack of skill in the language, which was evident at his confusing some words with the others because he could not distinguish the length of the vowels.

At five o' clock, in the afternoon, after an exhausting day, the Peñon came back home with a loaf of French bread, which he had bought in a bakery in the centre of the town, under his left arm. The pastry was the aliment to mitigate his hunger at midnight, which always made his stomach membrane curl because of his very early dinners and small breakfasts. He didn't take lunch because of his scarcity of funds, so he had just two meals a day. Once he was in, the landlady let him know some changes. The lad respectfully took off his white beret, which made him look like a real Portuguese.

"Luis, I've changed the sheets."

He was frightened much by the last word. The lady of the house had to say it again because of the doubt expression on the Peñon's face.

"Luis, I've changed the sheets."

She had pronounced every word of the phrase with emphasis and gestures so that he could comprehend the meaning of each one of them. But his uncertainty did not abandon him.

The untidy woman, grabbing him by the hand, led him to the bedroom. While they were going upstairs, little drops of cold perspiration ran down upon the lad's grainy cheeks. Once they were inside, the landlady aimed with her coarse index finger at the unravelled white sheets. As the Peñon realized what she meant, a sensation of relief came over him. He had understood the word "shit", whose vocal "i" is short, in comparison to the "i" sound in "sheets". Because of this misunderstanding, the lad had interwoven in his realm of imagination a most shameful calamity about the landlady's non-existent motives to discard him onto the English streets. In his mind, he had pictured himself drowsing surrounded by his luggage in a park the whole weekend, since he could not afford a bed and breakfast.

21

The hilarious incident of his miscommunication with the landlady enlivened many occasions when his friends talked about. Its black humour was often the beginning comment to initiate a chat with the opposite sex, but unfortunately it did not arouse any reaction in females.

***

Soon the Peñon was abandoned to his eternal friend, solitude, once he had concluded his language course. The new college, located in central London, where the lad was doing his studies of tourism, was mainly attended by north European students, who were individualists and whose practices turned individualism into seclusion. What a pity! Nevertheless, a bright idea came to his mind to push away barriers: to be christened anew.

Jeremy Smith would be his Anglo-Saxon name. People questioned him about the origin of his new surname, which might well be attributed to southern United States because of the colour of his skin. The Peñon justified the fact that an "American" had poor English pronunciation by saying that his mother was from the Caribbean and that she had, at his father's death in the U.S., gone back to the Tropics, this time with her son, so that he was brought up over there. When he uttered the name -and this was not understood well- the

Peñon muttered to himself, "Jeremy Smith or something like that".

In the pages of the British Council's big book he found the college, which was not precisely Oxford, but the tutors were committed to imparting the basis of a solid education to those who were interested in having it. The structure of the place was something rare for the lad. Every floor had been divided into small lecture rooms. It was quite difficult for him to believe that a person like the director, with his loathsome, alcoholic look, and his vocabulary of just two words ("no" for whatever thing was asked, and "money" for everything), was a citizen of the first world.

As the first nine months went by, the Peñon had to endure the severity of God's punishment, inflicted on his descendents, the Lords of the Earth who liberated the minotaur and caused it to collide with astron stars, throwing ice fragments and exhaling the origin of the overpowering breeze that scourged men's defenceless back. For the first time, he had to wear heavy clothing. Though it was a torment, the fantasy of being a rock musician flourished in the lad's mind when he put on his leather jacket. His dream faded away, however, as sun light melts the snow, when the calor heater was not enough to warm up the big, damp room at night, and he had to lie down over the unravelled carpet and lean his back against the

23

footboard of the bed in order to be at the height of the lit grille of the portable device. The boring routine of using an iron to heat up the sheets was necessary to do before he slumped himself over the mattress. At midnight, he was disturbed by the unpleasant noises coming from the rickety chest drawers, where the night intruders put themselves up. The lad could not get rid of them because it was quite difficult to move out the furniture to clean it up, and the landlady gave no any help, only the response that rodent devoured no people. It was hard for him to pretend to be a rock star among the gloomy shadows of his room.

Somehow, on the other side of the endless tunnel of calamity glimmered a little flame, which did not last long. The people of the town had accepted the Peñon, and he noticed it daily when he came across acquaintances who greeted him on his way to the train station. Of course, their attention was brief, and it had taken him one year of his life to make even this progress. Despite everything seemed to go right, unpleasant moments could not be avoided.

It was Friday' night. As usual, the Peñon went to a disco, one of small dimensions, in the basement of a hotel by the sea front, to listen to Caribbean music, which he loved. This was his first time to be in a Latin place in a developed nation. He had chosen that disco in order to meet the opposite sex, because he supposed the

Oliver Frances

people of the northern globe didn't know how to move around to salsa rhythms. As the Peñon was pacing along the corridor inside the club, he observed three areas with architecture like catacombs where people were seated around tables, placed in the centre underneath a red light. The illumination reminded of the ill-famed bars of his country. On the other side of the dance floor was a roomy place, more illuminated and crowded with people chatting. The lad beheld the dancers who were opposite him until his eyes lighted on an attractive young girl. A ladies' man, the Peñon approached her, thinking she had no dance skills. The two went to the centre of the area, where he splayed his legs around, but his clumsy movements did not go at the same tempo as her correct dance techniques. His humiliation was over when she discarded him for being a terrible dancer.

The misfortune lad, humiliated, retreated to a corner of the disco, when the plumpish disc jockey met him.

"How are you?" the man asked.

"Fine," the Peñon answered. Then, observing the man's coarse Andean features, he asked. "Are you from South America?"

"Yes. From Peru."

"¿Y eso por aquí?" ("And what are you doing here?")

"Yo soy exiliado político. Por los momentos, estoy estudiando en Sussex University y, aquí los viernes por la noche por diversión," responded the DJ. ("I am on political exile. For the moment, I'm studying at Sussex University. I'm here on Friday nights, just for fun.")

The man uttered his words with an arrogant tone. His story did not arouse any suspicion in the lad, who was astounded by the man's merriment. Years later, the colours of the important picture the man had painted of himself would fade when the Peñon found him in the Social Service Office, in the unemployment section, and learned he had never enrolled any university. The man's story about his exile, which he told exclusively to foreigners, amused the lad in his sad hours. In spite of being a person of that sort, the man introduced the Peñon to a young lady.

Unexpectedly, the illusion of that woman, who might become the companion of his jubilant days and, in his most depressive hours, kiss his thick lips and fondle his cut-off hair, made his heart leap.

"What is your name?"

"Patsy, and you?"

"Jeremy."

"Where are you from?"

"From America, but I was brought up in South America. This is the cause of my accent."

"Really? What do you do here?"

"I'm doing a tourism course."

"And you, Pepsi?"

26

"It is Patsy, not Pepsi."

The Peñon was starting to think she liked him, inasmuch as she hadn't yet pronounced the famous words to end a chat: "See you later". It was a favourite phrase for the English; it evidenced their disillusionment about the person was opposite them. Patsy gave every impression that she was not upset with the harsh sound of the lad's pronunciation. She had even accepted his reason for it. Misfortune did not abandon him, however, and he kept mistaking the lady's name.

"Well, Pepsi."

"Look, I am not a drink. My name is Patsy. P A T S Y," told the young, annoyed.

"I'm sorry."

"See you later."

The lady didn't bother to telephone him in the following days to give him an opportunity to amend his mistake. It disheartened him so badly that he began to think that nobody would be interested in him in that part of the world. Nevertheless, fate put on his way a foreign lady, who did not care about his accent provided that his movements in bed were right.

For a year and a half, the Peñon applied all his efforts to completing the laborious task of procuring due linguistic adroitness in the English language. His studies contributed for it. About his romances, they were just like April showers. The Peñon's parents were jubilant at

27

hearing the news about their son's advance, about which they boasted in front of their relatives. For them, the Peñon was a living treasure. In spite of having a little bit of common sense, bad thoughts never left his mind in peace. And, instead of concluding his courses, which his parents went to great lengths to afford, and returning to his native land, where his girlfriend did not faint in her wait, in order to draw some benefits from what he had learned, the lad decided to abandon the college and search for a job, from which he would obtain enough funds to establish his own business, as the Italians had done in the Bronx. His business would be not in New York, just in the capital of the world: London. So, he went around to the fast food shops, run mostly by foreigners, and the pubs, nightclubs, shops and newsagents. The Peñon never gave the number of his passport to his employers, not even for a night with the English girl who turned him into jelly.

Fortune had been accompanied him in many occasions, but it soon snatched its protective mantle away from its beneficiary, and the horrible cape of unprotectedness was over the Peñon when he was employed as a cashier in a kebab restaurant, some distance away from his home. The nice words of the Turkish, the owner of the place, enchanted him, mostly because of the fact that his boss was a foreigner too. So he let open the petals of the flower of confidence

28

to embrace a new friend. Nobility was in it. Once the owner got the coveted passport number by his worker, extortion was the gratification for this marvellous brotherhood, which involved one of the Peñon's work friends -a South American too. Despite this misfortune, he was accused of stealing opportunities and women's heart.

The nefarious actions of the Turk didn't last long. In the meantime, the Peñon resigned to uttering the accurate phrase of the country for strangers: "Bloody foreigners". The blackmail ended when the Peñon, clasping a cook's knife in one hand and holding the Turk's neck with the other hand, thrust the man's face over the restaurant's frying pan and threatened to murder him if he continued the extortion. The intimidation was so horrible that the owner never dared to call the police. After that, laughter was the balm that healed the pain of being blackmailed, because the Peñon had defended a Venezuelan man: things would had been completely different if they had been on Latin American ground, where the two men would be at odds with one another because of the trespasses his country had committed to extract Venezuelan's riches.

The Peñon's ill–fated work experience had not discouraged him. With new wings, the lad started to look for another job, which he found in a nearby town. This time, he followed the celebrated rule of the Jewish proverb "Don't trust even your father".

***

The bothersome routine of making periodic trips abroad to renew his visa, since he no longer had his long-expired student pass concluded when love blossomed in a lady's heart for the Peñon. She would do the trick. The gods had not been so splendid with her, if she were compared with those women the lad had dreamt of -gorgeous cover models or those photographed topless on page three of the major circulation tabloid in the kingdom. She was not even so beauty as his Colombian friend, a sun-browned South American who had the most desired ladies about town. Nobody jested about her look, although she was similar to a globe rather than to a woman. Her careless appearance and shabby clothes were unremarkable, because her sort was normal in females in that part of the world. Somehow, her soul was an oasis in an arid desert, and she offered the brilliant opportunity for the Peñon to obtain his permit work as well. Without hesitation, the Peñon married to the Englishwoman. His parents didn't attend the wedding, and the Peñon lied to them telling that she had excellent physical attributes as qualities —a combination that was quite hard to find them in the third world. Before that, his mother

Oliver Frances

expressed her due congratulations and resigned herself to the fact of losing her beloved son. In this way, the Peñon got a labour stability and, perhaps, an emotional one too.

***

Every season impetuously went by as a light feather thrust by the robust wings of breeze, leaving marks on the Peñon's body and soul. His existence was a kind of Trojan horse that dealt misfortune and trampled on his hopes, and the Peñon had to fight so that he wouldn't die in the toughest war that was life.

The last lance stabbed in his heart was the misfortune of his business, which involved fast - or rather, ultra quick- food. Training was vital, so, using recipes his parents mailed him, he learned how to cook a traditional Jamaican dish referred to as "patty" in the South of London. Once he was apt to undertake it, he eagerly awaited his first workday, which lasted barely five minutes.

Grabbing the handle of a saucepan full of hot patties in one hand, and a camp stove in the other; the Peñon went to the town's centre. Before he had even gone a block, a well-mannered policeman, with his black outfit and oval-shaped helmet, stopped him.

"Good morning. Where are you going to with this saucepan and camp stove, sir?" the policeman asked.

"I'm going to the centre," the Peñon replied.

"What for?"

"To sell food."

"Have you got the permit for that?" The policeman demanded.

"No, I don't need it. It's free trade."

"I'm afraid not, sir. You need a permit to sell food on the streets. And a very special one to do what you want. Besides, let me remind you about the fact of that you can burn somebody with the cooker," the official warned severely.

The Peñon listened to the policeman astounded.

"Where do you live?" the officer continued.

"On this block."

"Well, go back home and put away this stuff. Otherwise, I will have to put you in prison," he ordered him lastly.

Authority's words to obstruct his private initiative were not the Peñon's only disappointment. England's rigorous legal system and taxes discouraged him also. After the patty incident, the Peñon considered that it was more beneficial to gain his daily bread as a carpenter, and, in the lean years, as a waiter in the café of an Iranian friend. Even though his beloved wife did not give a helping hand in that business, she was content with his decision.

He put optimism behind him.

***

The light hands of the clock of age crept on, and the Peñon, now mature, kept his ideas of development of the nations on his mind. A wonderful spring inspired discourse anew. On this occasion, his dull considerations were about the predominance of the great colossus of the north, on the other side of the Atlantic, and the contribution of each of the fifty states to the world. His sorrow was not to have chosen this country when he departed from his native land. His discourse was met with gross opposition from his Colombian friend, who was not like Mochito, who used to listen patiently to his foolish chat about the kingdom. The Columbian contradicted him, propping up the argument that the States was not the nation for the blacks because of racism. In a way, he said, it was similar to his born place, where keeping oneself alive and progressing in life were needed to have influential friends or become a member of a political party. It was quite distinct, in the land of the kings, which had granted him benefits, everything from a house to a pension on unemployment, and had treated him as a human being. The Peñon quietened himself down at hearing his friend's argument. Even so, his ideas still lingered, but in silence.

As the Peñon was having a walk along a street by the centre, he was busy meditated on his existence when the need of returning to his roots blossomed in his heart. Without any vacillation, he boarded a plane to South America, not with his beloved consort, for he did not wish to frighten his parents. For this reason, he told her that his mother was dying. Knowing her annoyance at hospitals, he told her it was best not to visit the Caribbean in this occasion. During the hours of the flight, every scene of the life of the lad who had departed from the Tropics to search for a new horizon came to his mind, and he heaved a sigh. At some feet high, he was able to observe misery, which had not changed. It was still worse. Everything was yet the same. Time had stopped in this part of the globe.

Once the Peñon emerged from the tainted glass doors of the customs office, his mother shed tears of emotion as she saw her boy, who was a kid no longer. His hair had turned grey and his straight, stout figure had turned to that of a withered hunchback. The bitter fruit of age was hanging over the man.

The colourful parish maintained its old style. The endless roads, spread out like a big, majestic chair, lingered between the ruinous ancient and modern architecture. The parishioners still had their notorious joyful mood, despite the calamities that scourged the country. The pretty girls threw rich aromas from their curved figures as they walked past the street corners. The whisper of the chats of the big ladies was a distant note of the musicality of their voices.

34

Oliver Frances

The bells of the church announced the beginning of the end of the day.

With a great enthusiasm, the Peñon encountered with his bosom friends, whom he had left in the full flourishing of his youth. Mochito was not a fragile boy any more; he had gained weight and turned himself in a prosperous businessman. He owned a chain of fast food restaurants in the city. The Peñon's pretty, dark girlfriend, whose hope withered during her long wait for his return, had married a young man with a promising political career, and she helped him daily. And, his others friends were struggling to have a better life in their country. The Peñon was the only one was running after an unreachable future as the failure of the world.

A brilliant rainbow of prosperity was arched upon their lives of his friends, as he was beholding it a small maggot of envy ate its way into the tempting apple which had been annihilated by the comparison of one world to another. Once more, his lips uttered foolish words, but this time they were about the great difference he had observed on the legislation of the first world as opposed to the third one. These differences were starkest in violations of human rights and corruption in -the basis of an inefficient political and economic system. The conclusion he had drawn from all these considerations was to migrate to the developed

35

nations to liberate himself from backwardness and all its inconveniences.

If any South American country wanted to reach some degree of development, it had to become an associated state of the colossus of the north as a Caribbean island did. This was his theory for the progress of South America.

***

During the fourth week of his vacation, the Peñon abandoned the Tropics to return to his bothersome life in the kingdom. This time, he was completely resigned to spending his days on the works he could do, using his abilities to live on the money earned, and with the companion had chosen for wife, tied to her not by love but by habit. To the past belonged his idle explanation upon his accent, which used to enliven moments in the pub, and the name of Jeremy, with which he would also christen his son -who would be a northern man. He heaved a sigh, knowing that it was impossible to turn back the hands of the clock.

The Peñon wished to have accepted the Caribbean coast, even the worst of its natural landscapes, to compose his discourse on advance.

Oliver Frances